EDWARD HUNT

UMAIR KIDWAI

Made with ♥ on the Notion Press Platform
www.notionpress.com

Dedicated to my Parents, Shuja Kidwai and Rehana
Kidwai

Contents

Acknowledgements   *vii*

1. Origin   1

2. The Team   16

3. Twisted History   33

4. Confronting Professor   41

5. Runar's Return   48

6. The War Of The Damned   57

7. Sir Edward Hunt   65

Acknowledgements

Big thank you to my uncle, Mohammad Hasan, for guiding me through the entire process of writing the book, from planning, to publishing and everything in between.

CHAPTER ONE

ORIGIN

The wind was howling through the city while singing its melancholy song. The sky was dull with mood-sickening clouds hanging oppressively low. A young boy was looking through the window of his house at the silent streets with no expression on his face while the condition outside was not making him feel any better. It's the sort of place where one could go mad due to the silence. Not a word, a car's horn or an infant's cry could be heard. There was no crowd or a bustling atmosphere. It was strange how a place could be so quiet even though there must be over fifty people living within half a mile's radius of Edward's house. Now that may not sound like many people, but it was to them, considering the size of Edward's locality. He just celebrated his sixth birthday. Edward Hunt was his name. Edward came from a middle-class family. Although he attends a government boarding school where most of the facilities are funded by the government, he lives alone in a small house with no siblings, pets, or other companions. Only his parents are present. He is sitting in his bedroom, gazing out his window at the noisy, congested streets. He is currently at his home enjoying a rest. In a week, he will return to reside in the school. Any travel would have satisfied

Edward's desire for adventure. Something to do instead of just staring through his window and moaning about how bored he is. Edward rose from his bed and left his tiny space. He entered his parents' bedroom.

"Mom, I want to go somewhere other than here, just for some time," Edward said calmly and monotone. His mother responded, "Edward, you know we are not earning much, so how can you expect us to go on a vacation?" She did, however, even want to take him on a trip at least once.

Edward went back to his room with a dejected look on his face. He removed a book from his cabinet after opening it. Before his father arrived home, he read it for 30 minutes. His father is an accountant and makes a respectable income, sufficient to meet their basic needs and a little extra."

"Dad, welcome home!" Every time his father gets home from work, Edward repeats this.

He responded in a tired voice, "Hey, Edward." The family sat down for dinner after his father changed into his new clothing. They ate a straightforward dinner of garlic bread and mushroom soup. They always ate a simple meal, but this was a typical supper.

When you finish eating, Edward, let's go to your secret room, said Edward's father.

When Edward finished his soup and bread, he and his father left the home for Edward's hidden room. A tiny cave, that was. The vines covering the rock covered the opening. There was barely enough space in the little room for 3 kids. His dad assisted in building a tiny shelf on the wall that held some of his books and one of Edward's action figures. There was a battery-operated bulb and some canned food in the corner.

"So dad, what brings us here?" Edward enquired.

"I believed you might be interested in learning a language from many centuries ago." His father answered, "Yes! I really want to." Inquisitive and animated, Edward questioned, "What is the name of the language?"

"It is known as Irtese (Er-teez)".

Then his father revealed a battered book. The book's crimson cover was about the size of a standard school textbook. "A Complete Guide To Irtese," the cover stated. He spent some time studying Irtese with his father. And the following day. After a week, Edward mastered simple Irtese and could read simple and some complicated texts.

Edward's father inquired, "So, Edward, what do you want to be when you grow up?" He responded, "Well, I'm interested in science, so definitely a scientist."

Do you enjoy attending boarding school?

"It's okay. Not much to say about it. The washrooms are filthy. And the food is so old it should show the 'produced' date in BC."

"I'm considering taking us on a trip, Edward. Where do you feel like going?"

"Australia!"

"His father grinned a little. He smiled and said, "I will see."

Edward and his father returned home, where they all went to bed. He took one more peek outside the window before closing his eyes and drifting off to sleep.

Edward peacefully slept on his bed until he was woken up when he heard strange noises coming from his parent's room. There was snarling and growling, followed by a shout that sounded like his dad's. With trembling legs, Edward got up from his bed and slowly made his way to his parent's room while trying to be as silent as possible, not to be seen by whatever may be making those snarling sounds. As he turned to look inside the room, he saw the most horrifying thing that he had ever seen. His face turned pale, his blood grew cold, and he froze. The bed was covered with blood, and the walls were painted red. He came across his parents—or what was left of them. A human-like figure stood behind them, although it wasn't a human. Its eyes were a fiery red color, and its fangs were pointed. The monster was blue, had no muscles, and hovered beside a sword. But the fact that it was devouring his mother frightened Edward.

The creature said in a growling voice, "Where is he?

"I'm not going to tell you anything," said his father weakly.

"Last chance," the creature questioned again.

"You'll never find out. Never!"

While raging, the beast cut Edward's father's head off his neck with his sword. He moved the blade so quickly that no one could have seen him do it. Edward Hurried to the door and fled the house. With its unnaturally keen senses, the strange creature heard the door shut. It approached the door to look for anyone outside the house. It did not want to be spotted by anyone else, so it remained in the porch's shade. Thankfully, Edward had already made his way to his "hidden room," quick enough not to be seen (or sensed) by the creature. Edward slumped onto a cushion and broke out in tears. He reflected on his parents and what he had seen. He eventually fell asleep deeply due to his condition while trying to discover who the 'he' was. The following day, Edward awoke later than usual. The leaves on the trees were gently blowing off due to the constant, slow wind. Without any friends or guardians, his world appeared to be a vacuum. The only option available to Edward was to walk the approximately three-mile distance to his boarding school. He got up, ate a can of fruits in syrup, and began walking to the school with a heavy heart and shaky feet.

Ten minutes later, Edward was still making his way to the school when, to his good fortune, a kind woman driving a car spotted him moving with a sullen expression. The woman approached Edward after exiting her car. She was a wealthy lady with a black hat on her head and an off-white robe embroidered with blue flowers.

"Child, where are you going? She questioned, "And why are you alone?"

He answered the second question,

"Do you mind taking me to Boarding Enhance?".

"Of course not; come one, get in the car, and I'll take you there immediately. What is your name, then?

"Edward, Edward Hunt."

"Alright, Edward. I am Melanie Rose. Why were you by yourself?"

I'm not feeling like telling you about it.

"Oh, that's okay, I see."

Edward arrived at the school 15 minutes later, but it was closed, so he was forced to spend the rest of the day under a large tree to provide him with some shade. He took a bite of the canned fruit and had the good sense to bring his bag. The following morning, Edward got up early to make it appear as if he had arrived with the other students.

Eight years later

Edward is fourteen years old. He dropped out of school a while back because he could not pay the fees alone. Edward spends most nights in the wooden cabin. He discovered an old mattress that had been put next to the trash cans and which was intended for permanent disposal.

The following day, Edward decided to sneak into one of the classes. It was very tough for him to blend in due to the number of children there. He only had to skip the first thiry minute of school which is when roll call takes place. Biology was the first class. Professor Wilkinson, a specialist in biology and ecology, taught biology at Edward's school. He is a male who is 68 years old and has a beard of a median length, black and white, slick-backed hair and always wears glasses, a brown-colored waistcoat with a white shirt underneath it, brown corduroy pants with a black belt and black leather shoes. The Professor had already begun the session because he had a fascinating topic prepared.

"All right, class, settle down please, today we will learn about various animal species. Although I'm sure you've all learned this in prior years, we'll do more in-depth research this year. Can we list a few creatures we are familiar with before we begin?" He spoke.

Now, the solutions began to flood in. While some respondents mentioned unique animals like salamanders or armadillos, others mentioned the more common ones such as lions and tigers. Edward was next to go. Edward questioned,

"Sir, what are your thoughts on otherworldly beings?"

Professor gave him an astonished expression as he gazed at him.

"Would you mind expanding on that?" he requested.

"Bloodthirsty beings that resemble humans but aren't." Professor took a breath and remained silent.

"Although it is entertaining to imagine mythical creatures," Professor said, "Science has not established the reality of paranormal beings. We do not consider them real."

He then resumed teaching his class. It was time for a break after an hour. Edward hurried through the halls to find a place where no one would see him, in hopes of hiding, but ran into Professor.

"Dear Edward, Come with me." He spoke.

He then led him to a room in the janitor's room concealed by a particular tile that could be removed. It exposed a hole. The two went through the hole after Mr. Wilkinson double-checked if anyone could see them.

As Edward descended into the depths of the hole, he found himself standing within what could only be described as a clandestine laboratory. The walls of this dimly lit chamber were adorned with papers, their edges curling slightly where they had been affixed. The atmosphere carried a sense of dreariness, as if the room held secrets that the very air dared not reveal. Dominating the centre of the room was a table, adorned with an array of scientific instruments and tools. Among them, a lamp cast a pool of light, struggling against the surrounding shadows. Another lamp clung to the wall, its illumination feeble against the lab's pervasive darkness. This was no place one would call 'well lit' or the 'ideal study'; instead, it existed in a state of intriguing obscurity.The room buzzed with a tangible sense of activity, the remnants of experiments and research that had woven a tapestry of intrigue across every surface. The scene spoke of untold secrets, a silent dialogue between the seen and the hidden. The air itself seemed pregnant with knowledge, as if it held its breath in anticipation of revelations yet to come. Intriguingly, the lab's very design was a testament to its intention to remain concealed from prying eyes. The shenanigans and enigmatic activities unfolding within these walls were shrouded in privacy, with the room itself serving as a guardian of the mysteries it contained

"Professor, this is incredible," said Edward, admiring the lab.

"I wanted to talk about the topic you raised in class today. concerning supernatural entities," the Professor said.

"Oh, that was just an unrelated inquiry I had, nothing serious," Edward retorted.

"Look, you are hiding something, I know that. I've spent a lot of time researching this, so I'm sure I can figure it out." Professor said in a slightly irritated tone.

"Alright, I'll tell you. It happened nine years ago. I was woken up by strange noises from my parent's room. Sounds of snarling and growling followed by a shout from my dad. I snuck out of my room and slowly made my way to the door of his room. I saw a beast of no regular size we are used to, with a blue body and sinister crimson-red eyes. It killed my father with a weapon; I think it was a sword. And it was floating next to it, under its control."

"That was a demon you saw. Possibly the only one on the planet, and the same one that attacked me. I used a pocket knife to cut off a bit of its skin. I arrived here with the skin sample and began my research and experimentation immediately. I concluded that the demon could regenerate after conducting a few tests.

Is there a way to put an end to him?

"There is only one way. You must use a weapon or a projectile to hit the demon's heart. The demon won't be able to regenerate in this manner. However, the demon's tissue surrounding the heart would be tougher the more robust it was.

"I can help you battle the devil. I can demonstrate how to assault him and penetrate his heart. What do you say, then? Do you wish to battle the devil or maintain your current way of life? He questioned Edward.

"I need you to educate me. Tell me everything you know about demonology. If that's a thing." responded Edward with a stubborn heart and powerful intellect.

"Also, was there anyone who has fought a demon before?"

"Yes, there was one man, the first to stand his ground against a demon. I don't quite remember his name. But he was a legend with extraordinary powers." remarked the Professor. "I also recall this prophecy. That someone will free the demons or something? I don't know. Alright then, meet me after school every day."

Edward spends most of his time after class with the Professor. He is learning a lot from Professor, and they have become very fond of each other. If he is not with the Professor, he is presumably in the library scanning the volumes in the demonology area (essentially the fantasy section). It includes books written by Professor so that someone who has experienced something similar to Edward and Professor reads it. Edward learns a lot from these novels, like the fact that there was a portal that led to a dimension that houses the most dangerous demons to exist. He just found that the sword he saw floating beside the beast was his weapon. The demon can manipulate it and make it move at high speeds. One day Edward and Professor were in the lab, reading the books on demonology, when Edward noticed a chest on a table in the corner of the room. It was made of black stone with strips of gold on the edges.

"Professor, what is in that chest over there?" he asked, "That is a secret which will be revealed to you when you are ready," Professor replied.

Edward was dying to know what was in there, but he would not dare to open the chest after what Professor had said. He also noticed a book on the same table. It was written in Irteze.

"And what about the book next to the chest? It's written in Irteze. What is it?" asked Edward.

"That was a gift from a friend of mine. It's very precious to me and I don't let anyone touch it."

Edward's curiosity was almost overflowing at this point. He just had to know what was in the book and the chest. But he knew he had to control it.

"Can you read Irteze?" asked Edward. "I'm still figuring it out," replied Professor

"My dad taught me some Irteze. Maybe I can teach you," said Edward in a joking manner.

"Some other time, kid," said Professor lightly.

The Professor told Edward that demons had been hunting humans for as long as he could remember, and it was time to stand our ground and fight back.

"Edward, it is time I show you the ways of fighting a demon. I will show you spells to keep the demon at bay or even weaken it. I haven't told you this yet. There was a portal that led to the demon world. However, it is destroyed. That's where demons originate from."

Edward's curiosity peaked. He never knew about this portal, and just the thought of one excited him. He could already see an adventure or a mission being assigned to him and thought about all the new things he would learn and see. But he also feared that this mission might very well be his first but quite possibly his last. After calming down, he asked:

"Is it possible for a new one to open up anywhere?" asked Edward

"It is rare but it is possible. A portal can open up in a place where maybe a massacre by a demon took place or a large disturbance caused by a demon, or anything related to that can also be a factor. All this is irrelevant right now." Answered Professor. "Now back to your training. I will train you physically. You will start doing physical training. To strengthen your muscles, endurance, and pain resistance. We will forge a weapon suitable for you. And how will we decide that? I will just show you some weapons and you will see which one suits you best. Sounds like a plan?" Professor said,

"It sounds perfect. So when do we start?" asked Edward.

"Now"

For the next two years, Professor trained Edward. He did two hours of physical training every day. Lifting, pushups, jogging, you get the idea. And he followed a strict diet with no cheat days. After each day, he was exhausted. More drained than ever. But he knew he had to persist.

After two more months of training, it is time for Edward to choose a weapon for himself. He will use this weapon for the rest of his life. He will unlock its powers and make it his own, an extension of his body.

"Here are a few weapons I managed to make. They are made of a special mineral found deep underground and that too in a very insufficient amount. It has a special property of slowing down the regeneration of a demon, even if it is a by a little," said Professor

"Then how did you find enough to make these weapons?" asked Edward. "I have connections," replied the Professor. "Right now, you have to choose a weapon from these five: A lance, axe, bow and arrow, war sickles, and dual swords."

"I want to start with the axe," said Edward

Edward held the axe, tried to swing it, and got it stuck in the wall. Nearby, students heard a loud bang. And rumors started to spread of a monkey in the janitor's room.

"Okay, not the axe," said Professor

"Yes, not the axe," repeated Edward

"How about you try the bow and arrow," said Professor

Edward held the bow in his left hand, and with his right, he loaded the bow, shot it at the target, and ended up shattering an empty test tube. He quickly put it back on the table. Finally, Edward chose the dual swords. With a heavy heart, he picked them up and swung them repeatedly. His form was perfect, and he immediately knew it was perfect.

"The swords, I pick the swords," said Edward

"Alright then, now that's decided, we should start training you to use the swords," said Professor

Edward was eager to learn how to use real swords. He had never even touched one before. Edward only took four years of relentless training to partially master learning how to use the dual swords. He learned different forms of sword fighting and different techniques and even trained on dummies while trying his best to balance his training with his school life, which seemed like an easy job at first, but Edward greatly underestimated the situation. He barely got enough sleep and was late for a few of his classes. Sometimes Edward felt like he was the best swordsman in the world, but one mistake was enough to humble him. Even after four years of tears, sweat and blood, he needed more time to become a master; Edward and Professor both know he needs at least a year or two more. But they don't have a year. They need to stop the demon before he harms any more people. According to Professor, Edward is twenty-one years old and ready to take on the demon.

"I have trained and guided you, and you have reached a relatively high level. You are ready," said Professor. "According to my research, the demon spends most of his time in these parts," he said, pointing at his map in three places. "I don't know which place exactly, but it's one of these three places. I only have a vague idea of the location. It is a thick forest, but I'm sure you will be able to handle it. Are you ready to embark on your first mission?"

Edward thought about it for a moment, and with a determined look, he nodded. "I'm ready."

"Here is a sheath. You wear it on your back, here let me put it on for you," said Professor as he put the sheath on Edward's back. Edward put his swords in the sheath. He looked like a real fighter with two sword handles on either side of his head and a long black coat with purple lining that Professor gave him.

"Edward, you must remember to stay sharp and alert at all times. The demon can be very sneaky and deceiving if you aren't paying attention," said Professor. "There won't be any backups, that's for sure, but still, just stay alert."

Edward bids farewell to Professor. Even after training him for five years, Professor was a little worried. He retreats to his courtyard and looks up at the orange evening sky. He murmurs something to himself, and a tear rolls down his eye as he watches Edward's silhouette become smaller and smaller.

Before entering the end of the city, he went to a local grocery store after hiding all his weaponry. There, he bought tinned food to feed him for a few weeks using the money Professor gave him. He also bought a lot of water bottles. He was lucky to find a caravan to take him to his destination. The driver was confused about why someone would want to go into the forest, feared by the whole city. Agreed to take Edward there as long as he was paid. By the end of the day, Edward had reached the end of the city and was now near the forest as marked on the map. The details on the map were almost identical to what he was seeing.

"Wow! Professor is a genius!" he thought.

Edward entered the forest. It was dark, and the place was shrouded with leaves. The towering trees block sunlight from reaching the ground.

He inspected the map and started with the leftmost path, which again divided into two more pathways. Edward chose the right one. He walked for three minutes and ran into a vast vine area. Edward unsheathed his sword and slashed each vine, blocking his path. He was getting too carried away cutting vines that he overlooked that he had walked right into quicksand. Edward started to panic. He struggled a bit, then took a few deep breaths. Edward wedged his sword into the ground, pulled himself out, and collapsed. He got back up, and this time Edward walked around the quicksand. Edward followed the map and reached the first point, a clearing in the forest. To his disappointment, he found nothing. Edward moved on. He had no time to waste. He walked for four minutes until he arrived at the second point and suspected nothing, but just as Edward was about to move on, he heard a rustling sound in the bushes. And then another in the trees. Edward unsheathed his swords and got ready to fight. Just as he thought he had found the demon, he was ambushed by four demons. Edward could not believe his eyes. There are more demons. Professor and Edward had been wrong this entire time. He took too long to think about the situation, and the demons had pinned him down. He broke free but was again trapped on all four sides. The demons pounced on him. He stabbed one in the chest and killed it, but the other three pounced on him and didn't let him move. With no time left to think, Edward panicked; even if the demons let him free, he would not move since he was frozen with terror and dread and felt a chill down his spine. Edward's life flashed before his eyes. He thought about Professor, his parents, and his old house. Edward had just begun his mission but had failed in less than an hour. Other than fear and sorrow, he felt disappointed in himself. He had let Professor down, and he was able to avenge the death of his parents. However, in a few moments, all his thoughts would be meaningless. Just as he thought he was about to die, he felt an arm grab him. He was quickly dragged away from the demons. He quickly got on his feet.

"Hurry, follow me, we have no time to lose," said the person who rescued Edward.

Edward shakily ran behind the man while stumbling and tripping along the way, and he led him to a small cave.

"Who are you?" asked Edward. "I am Ray Green," he replied. "You may not believe it, but I am part demon and part human."

CHAPTER TWO

THE TEAM

"I am Ray Green," he replied. "You may not believe it, but I am part demon and part human."

Edward could not believe what he had just heard.

"How can you be part demon and part human?" asked Edward

"I was attacked by a demon as well. The demon managed to inject some of its poison into my arm. For a few days, the pain was unbearable and I even thought of cutting my arm off," replied Ray. "I managed to get my hands on an antidote. Surprisingly, the demon's poison was a lot similar to snake poison."

"So what happened after you drank the antidote?"

"It was able to subside the poison, but since it had been in my body for a while, it was able to spread, giving me a few demon-like powers."

Edward never knew it was possible to be a demon and part human. Professor didn't mention anything about the same.

"I have been looking for people like you for eight years. Those who have been attacked by a demon and have trained to fight to fight one," said Ray.

"Why don't you join me? Also, I still don't know your name."

"I am Edward Howard. And yes, I would like to join you," said Edward. "I want to know what weapon you use."

"This is a staff," replied Ray as he pulled out a long wooden staff with a pointed tip made of metal from his sheath. Ray said that they need to eliminate demons from this world at any cost. They are a disease that will keep spreading unless someone is there to contain them.

"We can't do it alone," said Edward

"And that's why we will need a team. A team of at least five brave warriors with unique skills, speaking of which, what are you good at?" asked Ray.

"I am quick and I have fast reflexes. I have good deductive skills. I was able to complete my book of mysteries I had as a kid," replied Edward

Ray was a little impressed by his description; though it was brief, it was enough for Ray. After discussing more things, they may need more weapons and a good base hidden from others.

"I can take care of the weapons," said Edward. "But the base may be a bit of a problem."

"The base and weapons come later," said Ray. "For now, we need a team."

"Edward, I need you to scour for members you think are appropriate for the job while I search for a good location to institute our base," said Ray. "They should be aware of the existence of demons or should have a spirit to fight against them."

"How many people do we need?"

"For now, five including us. And we need a bulky one, someone who is good at long range attacks and one who is swift and silent. Like you."

"And where do I find them?"

"Two days ago, I went to check around the city for any signs of demons. I didn't find them but I found signs of a fight, and not any fight, the damage marks and scratches were not from a gun or a man, it was something else."

Ray told Edward a few locations where he might find someone who had seen a demon and bring those people back where they were. Edward set out for the city to find members for the organization, which is not an organization yet but will evolve into one. It was nighttime, and it was quiet. Finding even one member would be next to unattainable at night. That, too, knows about demons.

Edward checked every nook and cranny but needed help finding a single person. He decided to give up. Edward turned around and headed back to the forest. He heard a trash can fall on his way, followed by a peculiar snarling and grunting. And it wasn't from a bear or any animal Edward was familiar with. It was coming from an alley, a dark alley.

Being the curious boy he always has been, he went to investigate. As you step into the alley, the first thing that catches your attention is the cracked bricks that pave the way, creating an uneven and treacherous surface. The passing of time has taken its toll on the alley, leaving patches of moss scattered around the walls and floor. The lack of light adds to the eerie atmosphere, making it difficult to see what lies ahead. A puddle of murky water stands in your way every few steps, forcing you to tread carefully and watch your step. The overall impression is neglect and abandonment, with an unsettling feeling of being watched from the shadows.

Edward located the cause of the sounds. He was witnessing a demon attack. It was surprising enough for a demon to be in the city, but what was more surprising was that the man it was attacking was holding his ground against the demon. He was pushing it back and almost made it fall. The demon retreated a few steps to regain its balance and then pounced on the man, pinning him to the ground while drooling on his face. Before the man got hurt, Edward swiftly entered the fight and stabbed the demon's heart, killing it. It turned into purple dust, and poof, and the demon was gone.

"How did you do that?" asked the man, wiping off the demon drool.

"I could ask you the same," replied Edward. "How did you hold your ground against a demon?"

"Not to brag but, I never skip leg day, or hand day, or any day," said the man

"What's your name?" asked Edward

"I am Logan Brown."

Logan is muscular, strong enough to hold against a bull and at least eight inches taller than Edward.

"I am Edward Hunt. I am searching for people who have been attacked by demons or are aware that they are real. My friend and I want to gather as many people as we can to kill every remaining demon on this planet so that they can no longer pose a threat to humanity and I'm pretty sure that all three of us know the sort of powers they possess. I want to know if you would like to join us. We could use your strength to fight demons. " said Edward

"Who else is on this team?" asked Logan.

"Well so far only two people including me. If you want to know about the other one, you need to come along with me."

Logan took a moment to think about it, and realizing he didn't have anything better to do, he agreed.

"Alright, I will join you. But this is worth it. I'm risking my life doing this."

Logan followed Edward back to the forest. Edward returned to Ray's cave; thankfully, they found him there.

"You're back already? And with a recruit?" said Ray in disbelief, seeing that Edward had already found a new team member.

"Who's this guy? His face is annoying me. Can I punch him?" said Logan

"He's Ray Green. And probably the leader of this team," said Edward

"Probably? What do you mean probably?" said Logan

"We haven't decided on the leader yet."

"This team is hopeless," said Logan with a sigh

Ray got up, and before Logan realized he had made a move, he put his staff up to Logan's neck.

"Watch your tongue," he said

"Or not," said Logan

Logan jumped back. Ray is intimidating enough to make a man who could take on a bull flinch.

"So tell me about yourself. Your history, where you came from, and why you decided to join us," said Ray.

"I was raised by a family of farmers. I used to do a lot of farm work, which has made me a lot stronger than most. I worked there for four years. When I turned fourteen, my parents died at the hands of a demon. Since then I've been on my own on the streets. A demon would occasionally show up and I would do my best to hold it off. I joined you guys for two reasons. I hate demons and I was bored and sick of living in the streets, it's embarrassing," said Logan.

"Alright then. I know who you are and why you're here, but you must make a pledge."

"Anything," Logan said, relieved.

"Never give us up, never let us down and never desert us in any case," said Ray. Logan was perplexed with the framing of his words but understood what he meant by this and promised to do the same."Edward, you said you know where to get the weapons from, am I right?"

"Yes I do," said Edward

"Get all of them."

"There are four weapons and I won't be able to carry all of them."

"Okay. I will carry one, you carry one and Logan carries two."

All three of them set out to retrieve the weapons led by Edward. After ten minutes of walking, they arrived at the boarding school.

"We are going to have to be very quiet," said Edward

Edward took Logan and Ray to the janitor's room, where Professor's lab was hidden.

"You guys stay here," said Edward. "I will bring the weapons out here and then we'll take them back."

"Why can't we go with you?" said Logan with a bit of suspicion

"Don't question him," said Ray

Logan shut his mouth immediately. Edward entered the janitor's room and locked the door. He opened the tile and climbed into the lab. Professor wasn't there, so he picked up each weapon and brought them up individually. The lance and axe gave him a hard time, but that didn't stop him. He presented the weapons to Ray and then took them back, with Logan carrying the axe and the lance. They took it back to the cave.

"Logan, choose a weapon," said Ray

"Axe, the axe anytime."

Logan swung the axe and did it perfectly. Unlike Edward, it was the perfect tool for him; surprisingly, he got it on the first try.

"I guess it's time to find the fourth member of our group," said Ray. "Logan and Edward, Head out to find the fourth member. I almost forgot about the new area for a base."

Logan and Edward once again went to the city.

"Who do you think we'll find this time?" said Edward to Logan

"I hope it's someone strong and knows how to punch like a gorilla."

Edward shook his head and focused on the search.

"Hey, gorilla, I'm small and light so I'll search from the roofs of houses while you search from the ground," said Edward

"Don't call me a gorilla!"

Edward ignored him and swiftly made his way to the top of a roof and proceeded to jump and run on each one while Logan was not too far behind on the ground. Edward had become proficient in parkour from navigating through the forest occasionally. Jumping across houses and climbing to the top of places that are usually out of reach is easy for Edward. Edward and Logan had been running for at least twenty minutes, but their efforts were unsuccessful.

"How much longer are we going to do this?" asked Logan

"If we don't find anyone by dawn, we head back," said Edward

They searched for half an hour more; by this time, they had covered half the city. Just as they were about to leave, they heard a loud alarm coming from a shop about a quarter mile away from Edward and Logan. They quickly made their way through the houses and arrived at the source of the sound.

"Thief! Thief! Someone stop him!" yelled a shopkeeper

Edward and Logan had their eyes on the thief.

"Yeah! Someone daring! He's probably muscular and big like me," said Logan.

"Keep your mouth shut, we still need to capture this man."

Logan got annoyed and almost swung his axe at Edward. They had caught up to the thief without him knowing. He was hiding in an alley. The thief had stolen a packet of chips and a drink. Edward jumped off the room, and Logan ran in from the other side. The thief was ambushed. But he ran right past Edward without him noticing. They were stunned by his speed. More so, he did it so quietly that Edward didn't even feel a change in the wind. Logan then stepped right in front of Chris.

Now he was trapped; Edward pointed one of his swords at the thief. He was very feeble looking and looked malnourished. He had short black hair and was an inch taller than Edward.

"This guy robbed a store and outran police? He looks so feeble," said Logan in disappointment.

"Why did you steal from the store, tell me the truth," said Edward.

"You won't believe me. But I'll tell you anyway," said the man. "My parents were killed by a demon when I was fourteen. And I've been living on the streets ever since."

Edward and Logan looked at each other, knowing the man in front of them was precisely the sort of person they were looking for, then looked back at the man.

"Hey, if you join us, you will be able to escape the police and take revenge on demons," said Logan

"I would love to but you annoy me. And you look like a gorilla."

Logan, sick of being called a gorilla, attempted to throw punche at the man. He dodged it, and to Logan and Edward's surprise, The man hit Logan back and hurt him. Logan was on the ground. Edward was speechless.

"What's your name?" he asked

"Chris Foster."

"I am Edward Hunt and the guy you punched is Logan Brown. And yes he does look like a gorilla."

Logan got up, and Edward led the way back to the forest.

They made their way back to the cave. But Ray wasn't there. The only thing they saw was a note. It read, "Hello Edward or Logan; If you are reading this, I am not at the cave. I am searching for a place to set up our base. If you find more recruits, show them the weapons and let them pick one. From Ray."

Edward followed the instructions and presented the weapons to Chris.

"Pick one," he said.

Chris said he is horrible with bows and arrows, and sickles are light and easy to use, so that's what he chose.

"Okay, time to find our last member," said Logan

Chris was testing his sickles and threw them right next to Logan. Thank god he missed it.

"Hey watch it!" said Logan, infuriated.

"Hey, look, the sickles come back to me when I throw it!" Chris ignored what Logan said. "Hey don't ignore me!"

"Chris, we're leaving," said Edward. "Logan, quit your screaming and come quickly."

The three were making their way toward the city. Chris and Logan were on the ground, and Edward ran through the trees. Edward was surprised that Chris was able to keep up with them. After all, he had outrun the police.

"Logan, hurry up," said Edward.

"Hey don't tell me what to do."

"Even Chris is outrunning you."

Upon hearing this, Logan ran as fast as a car. Chris was frightened. Logan outran Edward, but Edward wasn't giving up so soon. He increased his speed, and Logan was neck and neck. Chris joined in as well as was a little ahead of Edward. Edward sped up and was ahead of the other by a lot.

Just as they began to enjoy their little race, They heard a scream from the forest. They ran towards the location and saw three demons surrounding a girl no older than twenty. She had long brown hair and was an inch shorter than Edward. Each man took one demon. Logan first fought the demon with his fists. He was able to break one of its bones. But the demon regenerated.

"Logan, Chris! You need to damage the demon's heart!" said Edward.

Logan pulled out his axe and sliced the demon's body in half, turning it to dust. But it took at least half a minute. Meanwhile, Chris threw a sickle through the demon's chest, and it turned to dust instantly. Edward's demon took forty minutes. Edward remembered one of his lessons, the stronger the demon, the more time it takes to turn into dust. But this was not the time to think about it. They had to tend to the girl.

"Hey, I'm Edward Hunt. Who are you? And how did you get here?" asked Edward.

"I am Tara Winstone. Three years ago, my parents were killed by a demon inside my house. My parents were rich and well known, so their death caused a lot of controversy and people started blaming the government for their death and thought they were hiding something. I decided to stay quiet about it, it would just complicate things. I now regret that decision. I took refuge inside the dense forests and I have been living here since then. I was a profound archer, never missed the bullseye, so naturally, I took my bow and arrow with me before leaving to fend for myself. Though, one night, it was taken by a pack of wolves."

"Do you want to take revenge on demons?" asked Chris.

"Yes, I would love to."

"Then join us."

Tara thought about it for a while and agreed to join them.

"At least it's better than struggling for a little shelter," said Tara.

They went back to the cave and saw Ray waiting for them.

"I see you have found two more members. And good news, I found the perfect spot for a base as well," said Ray

"Tara, do you like archery?" asked Edward.

"Not to brag, but I am a skilled archer," said Tara.

"Good because you don't have a choice anyway, here's your weapon, a bow and arrow."

Edward asked Tara to tell him about herself. Tara said she was born into a wealthy family and started archery when she was eight. She was top in her class then and had a deadly aim, making the bow and arrow the perfect weapon for her.

"Ray, show us the spot you found," said Chris.

Ray led the way. Ray and Edward ran through the trees while the other three were on the ground. They ran through trees and pathways, twisting here and there. It was challenging to look around. It was a miracle how Ray never lost his way. After running and jumping, Tara got stuck in quicksand. Ray jumped off the tree he was standing on and stretched out his staff. Tara grabbed onto it, and Ray pulled her out with the help of Logan.

"As a trained archer and soon to be killer of numerous demons, quicksand shouldn't really be an obstacle for you," said Edward.

"I don't have much experience ya' know," replied Tara.

They covered a little more distance through the thicket and arrived at a small clearing in the forest.

"Here we are," said Ray.

"There's nothing here," said Tara

Ray shook his head and went into an area covered in thick vines growing down the branches of trees. Ray called the others toward him, and he disappeared into the vines. The others followed him. They were caught off guard and slid into a large hole. They all screamed and landed on a pile of leaves set by Ray. They took a moment to get up, and what they saw was astonishing.

Emerging from the tunnel, the team found themselves in a breathtaking expanse—the sprawling embrace of an underground world bathed in the ethereal glow of sunlight, using small cracks in the ceiling to creep inside the cave. The very air seemed to shimmer as they stepped into a vast underground cavern, a realm of wonder concealed beneath the earth's surface. Above them, the ceiling soared to astonishing heights, a canvas of raw, jagged rock adorned with stalactites that glistened with moisture. These geological formations hung like frozen tears, each one a testament to the silent passage of time. Beneath their feet, the floor unfolded in an uneven mosaic, a textured landscape punctuated by stalagmites that rose like jagged teeth, reaching for the unseen sky. The play of light and shadow cast by their headlamps danced upon these natural sculptures, painting a masterpiece of stone and shadow. Amidst this subterranean symphony, A small water hole nestled at the cavern's heart. This miniature oasis, cradled by the earth's embrace, promised sustenance. Fed by a natural spring, its crystal-clear waters gave the impression of a life-giving elixir, a tangible connection to the very heart of the earth. As if painted by an artist's hand, a cluster of trees adorned the cavern's edges. These arboreal sentinels, with trunks that seemed to touch the very roots of the world, thrust their gnarled branches skyward. They bore the gifts of nature—wild fruits, their colors vibrant and alluring, dangled temptingly within easy reach.

"Ray, it's perfect," said Edward.

Ray didn't say anything; he was in a corner, just standing there menacingly. It almost scared the others, but he was admiring the cave again. Everyone else made themselves busy finding a spot for themselves. Logan wanted a soft bed, so he chose an area with moss and grass growing around it.

"Don't even try to take this spot, it's mine!" He said.

Tara chose a large ledge not too high off from the ground. She liked to jump around and swing from place to place, so she naturally liked this spot. Edward and Chris chose the most generic spot: a flat rock with moss growing on it, like a mini plateau.

"Okay boys and girl, we need to make rules and then assign roles to each member. First, we pick a leader," said Ray

"You're the leader," said the other three referring to Ray.

"Well I guess that's decided, now for the rules," said Ray. "Number one: Never reveal your face to the outside world, you will be given masks to wear when you are on duty. Number two: Never act recklessly. Number three: Do your best not to make a scene. Number four: If you do make a scene in public, flee. Number five: No partnering with a demon."

"Where did you find time to list all these rules?" asked Edward.

"When you went to find Logan."

Ray said that the members had to learn how to fight. Since Ray, Edward and Logan already know how to fight, that only leaves Tara and Chris.

"Logan, you teach Chris and Edward, you teach Tara," said Ray

Logan complained about his partner but was immediately silenced by Ray. Logan taught Chris fighting stances and tricks. He made Chris do rigorous training, lifting weights, exercises, and more. On the other hand, Edward taught Tara to be stealthy and not make a lot of noise while carrying out missions. Tara already knew how to use the bow, so Edward ignored that. He taught her hand-to-hand combat in case she had to use it. Tara and Chris did not find it easy, they didn't like early morning workouts, and Logan ensured he did not go easy on Chris.

After every day, before going to sleep, Tara and Chris's limbs could not function normally, but they knew they had to continue with this. Logan and Edward weren't confident in their quality of teaching since they had no experience. Edward, who was trained personally by Professor, was able to provide better training to Tara and also helped out Chris and gave some excellent advice which he received from the Professor. After four long months of training, Chris and Tara were not masters but were much better than they were not long ago.

"Okay team, now that we all can fight demons and know basic fighting skills, it's time we complete our quest. Which is killing the demon who attacked Edward and me," said Ray.

"So how do we find this demon?" asked Tara.

"After some exploring, I found out that the demon spends most of his time in this spot," said Edward pointing to his map.

"If you know where it stays and you are so skilled, why didn't you attack it?" asked Logan.

"It's too strong even for me. That's why Ray and I formed this team, we can't fight demons alone."

Ray explained the rest of the plan and how to ambush the demon to the team. There will be risks, and they may lose someone, but that is inevitable. Ray assigned each person a role. Since Edward has good hearing skills and is very alert, he will warn anyone if demons are nearby. He will be behind Ray. They both will be in the trees. Logan, Tara, and Chris will be on the ground. Tara will be in the front, Chris in the middle, and Logan in the back. Tara will take care of anything in front. Chris will be back up and take care of the middle, and Logan will take care of the back. Everyone wanted to hear about Edward's experience fighting the four demons and being ambushed by them. He explained that one person does not stand a chance against more than one demon unless that person is very skilled and experienced; they have to stick together. If one person is captured, it should be their priority to rescue that person; they can not afford to lose even one man.

"A demon will try to pin you down or immobilize you somehow to make it easier to attack." Said, Edward.

They then set out to capture the demon. Ray led everyone to the demon's hangout. Again, Ray and Edward were jumping through trees, and the rest were on the ground. The group ran for a while, finally reaching the spot, and they saw something horrifying: three to four bodies bleeding out. They all had the same expression. The one you make when you go through a traumatic event. They investigated the scene then Edward climbed to the top of a tree to get a better view. He saw the demon in a clearing not far from where they were. He went back down and alerted the rest of the team, and they all followed Edward; soon enough, they found the demon. The demon didn't see them, or that's what they thought because the demon charged its sword toward Ray, but Edward blocked it with his sword. The demon didn't see that Tara had hidden in a tree beforehand.

She shot her arrow, but the demon dodged it just in time. The demon spotted Tara and made his sword fly toward her. She had no way of avoiding it. In time, Chris changed its trajectory by throwing one of his sickles. Ray charged at the demon with his staff and almost impaled its heart, but the demon dodged again. He used his sword to cut Ray's staff. He was weaponless. Logan charged at the demon and held it down so Edward could kill it, but it broke out of Logan's grasp.

Everyone was shaken. The demon charged its sword at Logan and almost got his neck. He dodged with a scratch and a bit of bleeding from it. Edward went for the heart but cut its arm instead. It instantly regenerated. The demon punched Edward and sent him flying; a tree stopped him and nearly broke his back. Chris threw both sickles, but surprisingly, the demon caught them and returned them. Chris dodged one, but the other got stuck in his arm.

He let out a small scream. The demon got distracted and didn't notice that Tara had released her arrow. It struck the heart. The demon immediately fell to his knees and slowly started turning to dust. The team celebrated for a few seconds but then noticed Chris under a tree holding his arm. Ray tied his arm with a cloth, and Logan helped him walk. They all headed back to the base. Just as they were about to leave the clearing, the demon spoke. "My name is Ryu. You killed me because you thought I was pure evil," said the demon. "But humans and demons have a long history, none of you know."

CHAPTER THREE

TWISTED HISTORY

The demon was tied, so he couldn't move. The team took a second to examine the demon. To make sure he didn't have any other tricks up his sleeve. They had a discussion as to what they should do with the demon. One suggested they should leave it here, as they can't trust their enemy, but the other said he could hold some information and they should interrogate him. All this led to an argument, but it was interrupted by the demon when he said:

"My name is Ryu. You killed me because you thought I was pure evil," said the demon. "But humans and demons have a long history none of you are aware of."

Upon hearing these words from the demon, the team froze. Logan almost dropped Chris. Ray turned to the demon with a severe look on his face.

"What do you mean?" asked Ray.

"I'm one of the strongest demons in the world. But somehow, you all managed to kill me. If I'm going to die, I will first speak the truth about this prolonged war between demons and humans," said the demon in a soft voice.

The team gathered around to hear what he had to convey regarding this war. The demon was slowly turning to dust, very slowly. He had enough time to tell them about the war. The demons started to speak.

"It all started three hundred years ago. Demons and humans used to co-exist. They did not work together but had no problem living with each other. Although they didn't usually enter each other's civilizations, they never fought. They didn't live on the same planet; their homes were connected through a portal. They called it Runar. It was sitting on the top of a small mountain called Magni. It was ring shaped and about ten feet tall. The portal was blue with swirls emerging from the middle, creating a spiral shape, and was outlined with a stone ring with blue stones on it. On either side of the portal were two pillars made of stone with runes glowing blue. In front of the portal was a small platform made of stone with curved blue lines. It was beyond science itself.

The first human to set foot on the rock platform could not grasp what he saw. The platform felt surreal, almost as if it was floating. A magical feeling would encompass anyone visiting the shrine for the first time. You could experience an emotion like excitement or something of the sort. Around it were many plants and flowers blooming, creating a lush environment.

Runar connected the human and demon worlds, but the environment in the demon world was so harsh and hostile that humans could not survive there. However, demons were able to enter the human world. Demons brought new technologies and knowledge to humans—contraptions they had never seen before. The humans realized they could use this technology to make their lives easier. They agreed with demons. The demons will supply humans with their tech, and in return, humans will allow them to cross the portal and live in the human dimension if they wish. Demons also agreed to share their literature and other intelligence documented over the years. Humans also shared their art, like pottery, paintings, and sculptures, showing their culture.

Everything was going smoothly. However, after living together for so long, some humans had evil intentions toward the demons. A small group of people had formed a secret organization hidden from the government and whoever was not a member. They operate very quietly without gaining any suspicions. And this organization is young. They had been running for two hundred years, gaining intelligence and planning their final goal, which is the sort of stuff you would hear in movies. Their final goal was to overpower the world. And they had been progressing at a very concerning rate.

Their spies were planning conspiracies and transferring their knowledge to the next generation. They shared their plans, charts, diagrams, and notes only with the children of the organizations and then with their children, and it continued. After the previous generation was out of commission, the next generation picked their next Leader.

They secretly hung out with demons at their base of operations, located a kilometer from Runar. It was a large area, more extensive than a mansion. It was underground and concealed by the lush vegetation around it. And no one ever bothered to explore that area anyway.

One day, a spy was out on a mission, their usual mission, which was to sneak into the government building with the help of a few demons who wanted to work with humans for world control. The government building is restricted only to authroized personnel. This place held all the information they had on demons.

The spy snuck into the building and crept into the main chamber. Agents heavily guarded the room. Luckily, they had memorized the shift timings, and the spy knew when the guard could not see him entering the chamber. He dashed inside. It was a small area, no bigger than Professor's lab. The spy took down notes and copied charts and diagrams.

Before leaving, he noticed a peculiar book in a corner. It was purple with text written in gold. He took it back to the base and presented it to The Leader. He inspected the book. He could not believe his eyes. It was a book of spells that could control demons. It was brought back to the base of operations.

The Leader of the organization took the book to his private lair, where no one was allowed to go inside. He spent a day reading it and trying to understand what the mysterious book comprised. He read about the powers of demons, where they came from and when they emerged. He read about their history, fights, wars, and ways to counter one.

But the most intriguing thing he read about was a particular mineral with excellent properties and stored great energy. A day later, he went outside his lair with a transformed countenance and a nasty look in his eye. Yes, he is evil, but he looked more sinister now.

The Leader walked into the main room, where humans and demons would discuss important matters. He walked to one of the demons. Everyone was watching The Leader with great curiosity. The Leader approached a demon and revealed a peculiar relic made of stone with carvings etched onto it, forming a diamond shape with a piece of amethyst inside. He held it at the demon and chanted a spell.

The relic started to glow with a purple light emitted by the piece of amethyst. It floated just above The Leader's hand and started spinning so fast that no one could tell it was spinning. The humans and demons took cover, scared it might blow up, but for some reason, the demon in front of The Leader did not move. Instead, it was blankly gazing at the relic.

A moment later, the demon started disintegrating and was sucked into the relic. Every witness was horrified but also amazed by what they saw. After the relic had calmed down, they saw the demon trapped inside it, trying to break free. The other demons, horrified by what they had seen, fled. But two demons were caught and brought back inside the base. Humans had acquired a power never meant to be in their hands.

With his men, the Leader went to Magni and climbed it intending to get to Runar. When they reached the top, The Leader performed another spell he saw in the book. He chimed in with various words which were in an unknown language. The ground started to shake, almost causing a rockslide, then the blue lines on the floor started to flicker, then died out, and then the portal started making funny noises and progressively shrank until it was closed. "For a new world!" said The Leader in a voice so loud and ecstatic that it could probably be heard for miles. Meanwhile, the few escaped demons hid deep inside the forest, where they found a small hole. They stayed there since they knew the four demons had no chance of fighting against humans with a deadly power at their fingertips.

The humans had no competitor or rival after closing Runar and obtaining a deadly power. No one could equal their power. They overthrew the ruling body and usurped the throne. Then proceeded to trap demons one by one using the spell. Their intentions were unknown, but it was immoral. This marked the commencement of what appeared to be an eternal dominion.

The people respected The Leader out of fear. They weren't fearful of him; they were scared of the book he had obtained. Although the spell was tested only on demons, they didn't want to take chances. They enslaved other humans. For what work, you ask? The Leader read about a unique gemstone called parasium, which he wanted to get his hands on. It had a quirky property.

When exposed to demon radiation, which is minscule energy produced by demons, it will absorb some of it. Parasium can store the radiation for later use, such as infusing it with weapons to give them special abilities or be used as an energy source. Only five grams of demon radiation-infused parasium could power the average household for eight months.

If The Leader could get his hands on this mineral, he could power contraptions deemed impossible to build or create weapons that were heard of only in tales and epics with powers never imagined. He tasked humans and some demons he had trapped to mine parasium without payment. Now you may be wondering why they would continue working. If someone disobeys The Leader, he will severely punish them, not whips or torture, but death (most of the time). Fear will keep them in line.

After eight days of ongoing and exhausting mining, someone had found a piece of parasium not more extensive than your little finger. He kept it in a satchel and brought it to The Leader. The Leader spent a few seconds turning it around and admiring it. Then he reached out for a hammer.

He kept it on a table next to the parasium. He flipped through the book, found a spell, and chanted it. The parasium emitted purple light, and a spiral of light engulfed the hammer and lifted it. The parasium slowly inched towards the hammer and the two fused. After the fusion was complete, the hammer had transformed from a golden weapon with blue engravings to a purple and black-ish hue with the piece of parasium stuck to it. The Leader went to the forest to test the new hammer.

He struck it on the ground and instantly cleared a path in the forest. And not any minuscule path. This one was at least three hundred meters long. The vegetation had all been uprooted and flung far away for anyone to track it.

The only thing remaining was the elongated crater that formed right before their eyes. Everyone present at the scene was astonished by the immense power of what was once a simple hammer, only capable of cracking titanium. After seeing what such a tiny amount did, he and all his men returned to the lair, hoping to obtain more parasium.

Meanwhile, the demons still hiding found a piece of paper that was blown away when The Leader tested his new hammer. The paper read, "After the great power is unleashed, they will rampage for years while trapping more. Then one day, a child will be born, who will free the enslaved." Let me break it down for you. The incredible power is referred to as the parasium. "They" refers to The Leader and his army. The boy is a mystery, and the enslaved refers to the demons he had trapped. This was not any ordinary sentence; it was a prophecy.

Fast forward to three thousand years later, the empire had finally fallen. How? Well, not even parasium-infused weapons can stand against nature. The empire suffered a great famine. Thanks to the excess number of rodents eating away the food stored for the winter without anyone noticing. If that was not bad enough, a mighty earthquake hit the heart of the empire, where a significant chunk of the work was done, and where the knowledge and tech were stored.

They had an entire empire to feed and rebuild the most important part of it. Not to mention all the information and tech they had lost. This was terrible news for the empire.

Since they had suffered such a significant loss, smaller countries took over parts of the empire bit by bit until nothing remained. Years later, a child was born, not just any child.

This child was the one that was stated in the prophecy. And it was none other than Sir Edward Hunt. The news was spread to the demons. They were delighted with this news and appointed a demon to find this child. They had appointed Ryu. Ryu was a skillfull war demon. Ryu set out to find this child and bring him to the demons. And that same night was when Edward's parents were killed, the moment that changed his life.

(Flashback over)

Ryu dies in front of the team. His final words were: "Please free our kin who have been trapped for millennia."

Edward made a shocking realization. Professor was the last of the lineage who trapped demons. He had been brainwashing Edward so that he could keep the practice alive.

"Ray, it's time I introduce you to someone," said Edward.

CHAPTER FOUR

CONFRONTING PROFESSOR

Ryu dies in the hands of Edwards after telling the team about the long history between demons and humans, but Edward makes a shocking realization.

"Ray, it's time I introduce you to someone," said Edward.

"What is his name? And why?" asked Ray.

"His name is Professor Wilkinson, but I call him Professor," replied Edward. "He is an expert in demonology and I am guessing he holds all the solutions to our troubles."

Ray asked Edward to show him the way to his lab so that they could confront him.

"If he's annoying can I punch him?" asked Logan.

"No, he's old. And don't just go punching anyone," said Edward

Edward led the way back to Boarding Enhance. Through the dark and empty streets when night arrived. They crept so no one could trace their steps. After running and hiding in between, they arrived at the school Edward grew up at. He had a feeling that the Professor would be in the lab somewhere.

They made their way through the silent hallways, almost ghostlike hallways of the school and once again, the team entered the lab, and as expected, Edward found Professor. They all ambushed him. With one of his swords pointed toward Professor's neck, Edward spoke.

"We know everything. Ryu told us every detail. Give us the book," Edward said sternly, almost scaring the Professor. "I knew you would find out some way or the other, but I wasn't expecting it this way," said Professor. "So you and your team managed to kill Ryu, and now you want the book. I won't give it up so easily."

"Don't be a crazy old man, this is a whole team, you're clearly outnumbered," said Logan in his typical arrogant voice.

"And I am the last man of a mighty lineage who could trap demons. And just so you know, this works on humans as well," said Professor.

Right after saying these words, he leaped for his main desk with all his books scattered across it, grabbed a drawer, and produced a key from his coat pocket to unlock it. Just then, Tara shot an arrow straight at Professor's head. He dodged it perfectly and unlocked the drawer. He pulled out a purple gemstone. It was parasium! He started to chant a spell, but Logan landed a hard punch on his right arm, and Professor fell into the wall. Chris tried snatching the piece of parasium, but to their surprise, Professor kicked Chris's leg and knocked him off balance. He then grabbed a staff on a bookshelf beside him and swung it at Ray.

He blocked his staff but was struggling to hold his ground. Then Edward came in and swung his sword at Professor. Professor dodged it but barely. A piece of his fantastic beard was chopped off (noo). Finally, Chris jammed one of his sickles into his leg, and Professor fell to the ground. The team tied him up and then proceeded to open the chest. Inside it was the Book of Spells. "If you open that book, it will bring nothing other than catastrophe," warned Professor.

They opened the book, ignoring the Professor. They saw the most confusing jumble of words they had ever seen. However, Ray can understand since he is part demon. He tries to recite one of the verses. He copies the text in the book and chants it. They all hear voices around the room. They weren't sure what they were but drew their weapons out immediately. The demons who had been in hiding for all those years were alerted. The book was awakened.

The team left the room with the Professor tied up. He looked at Edward and was astonished by how much he had grown. The team left the chamber and was outside the school. While outside, the Professor rolled to the other side of the room where his desk was. Under the desk was a button. But you could easily miss it because it blends into the table.

He pushed the button, and two staff members entered the chamber after a minute. These were people trained by Professor just in case something happened to him.

The staff members untied the Professor. Meanwhile, outside the school, they were about to return to their base when confronted by the demons hidden in the cave. They were startled, and they all pulled out their weapons.

"We are not here to hurt you," said one of the demons.

"We have been hiding in a cave ever since he came into power." "And who is this "he"?" asked Tara.

"We can not say his name. He is the one who imprisoned millions of our kind. He is the one who used Parasium."

Ray knew who they were talking about.

"So why are you here?" asked Ray

"We are here for the book. We need to free those in captivity." Ray sent Tara and Chris to check on Professor. They made their way through the hallways and found the chamber.

They entered it, and to their surprise, Professor wasn't there. Instead, they found the two staff members. And they could fight. They pulled out one sword each. One charged at Tara, and the other charged at Chris. Tara shot the sword right out of his hand with her arrow while Chris threw one of his sickles at the sword and broke it, then threw the other at his arm. Without caring for the staff members, they casually exited the chamber and immediately returned to Ray. They wanted to alert him that they couldn't find Professor anywhere, but when they got there, they saw Ray, Edward and the demons fighting him.

Professor was going to lose. The odds were against him.

The team, along with the three demons, were fighting Professor. Edward and Ray were using their weapons to push Professor back inch by inch until Logan ran past them and leaped toward the Professor. However, a man like him wouldn't fall for this attack. He dodged it and hit Logan's leg with his staff, causing him to turn mid-air and land on his head.

Edward then charged forward with his swords and swung them continuously at Professor, but all his attacks were dodged.

Since they were evidently struggling to land a single hit on Professor, he seized the opportunity and went for the demons. He was about to impale them when Tara shot an arrow at him just in time, but the arrow seemed different this time. The arrow left a trail of purple light, moving a lot faster; in fact, it was so fast that even Professor could not dodge it in time. It hit his left arm.

The moment it hit, it spread something inside his body, most likely a poison, he and became paralyzed. Everyone was surprised at what Tara did, including Tara herself. Ray said it was an extraordinary move which is very difficult to unlock, and it was a miracle that Tara could do it.

Since everyone was distracted by Tara's new power, Professor nabbed the piece of parasium from Chris and chanted a spell. The ground started to shake, and Professor's eyes turned purple. His hair started floating a little bit as if the energy was overflowing. Next, everything went pitch black. A moment later, when they could see again, they were pushed away with such force that Chris managed to break through two walls. But that wasn't all. Everyone's energy was drained out. They could barely stand up.

Professor advanced toward Ray, who was holding the book with the intention to take it from his hands and seal it away permanently until Chris reached for one of his sickles and threw it at Professor. Since Professor was so focused on reaching the book, he let his guard down and the sickle was jammed into his leg. He fell down in pain with a bleeding leg. And the team, along with the demons, left him there and left to complete the primary mission. Edward turned back to get a last glimpse of Professor. He was saddened by the fact that Professor was fooling him this entire time.

Ray decided it was a good idea to open the portal The Leader closed thousands of years ago. The one gateway that would allow the demons to finally reach their home. But the main task was to reach Magni. And it wasn't anywhere close to them.

The demons were the only ones who knew the way to Magni, so they were chosen to lead the way there, and the journey would take them about one day and one night on foot.

Ray sent Chris to gather food so they can maintain their strength. Tara was given two large water bottles by Ray and Edward, who conveniently had one with them. She was sent to find water from the lake in the cave. Edward, Ray and the demons were planning a route to reach Magni.

The book included a map of the area from thousands of years ago. They figured out where they were, and it was not easy, due to the fact that the book is millenia old. Of course, the demons also helped, and they contributed a lot since they posessed greater knowledge in this case.

They found a route that was not too difficult to go through and will get them there quicker than the other routes. It should take them about three days. They did take a while, but it was worth it. And by the time they were done, Chris had found a dead deer, and thankfully, it wasn't rotting. He cut out a portion of the meat and put it in a satchel that Ray gave him. He also found many strawberries and blueberries. Tara had collected water some time ago and just joined Ray and Edward to catch up on what they were doing. They only had to cook the meat that Chris had collected so that they could actually eat it.

Ray gathered firewood and dry leaves and brought them to the camp, and Edward produced some flint from Ray's satchel and lit the wood. Logan found a flat stone, so they cleaned it, placed it with water from the cave, put it on the fire, and then put the meat on the stone. Now they will have to wait for a while. After fifteen minutes, the meat was ready. They were ready for the long journey.

Ray assigned tasks to each person (and demon). Tara and Chris had to keep a lookout for any possible dangers. Logan had to carry the water and meat while providing support. His strength is inhuman, so it should be fine for him. Ray and Edward must always be alert because they are the first line of defense if they are attacked. The demons are in charge of navigation.

The tasks were assigned. Now they have to reach Mt. Magni. They had to go north-north-east, and their expected arrival time was one day and one night if they moved quickly with minimal breaks. After a little mental preparation, they began their journey. First, they speed through the forest. Ray, Edward and the demons were in the trees. Tara and Chris were on the ground with Logan a little behind them to keep an eye on things.

CHAPTER FIVE

RUNAR'S RETURN

Day 1

The team had crossed the forest through a route they had never taken before, leading them to a grassy plain with occasional trees that weren't as tall or bushy as the ones in the forest. They were already twenty minutes into the plains when they realized this was not an ideal spot for a demon to stay in as it was too open, so they had to do something to conceal the demons.

They had limited supplies and were surprised that this hadn't crossed their minds beforehand. They had no ideas, so they resorted to using their cloaks to hide them. (Each team member was given a cloak to hide their face and body if they had to.) It wasn't the best way to hide the demons, but it was their only option. The demons wore the cloaks and hoped they would not be seen. This place was completely empty, but they couldn't take chances.

The Team proceeded with their journey. They traveled for another two hours continuously, and it was getting dark, so they decided to call it a day. Edward and Ray found a madura cave with a roof elevated just enough for Logan to stand up straight. They decided it was best to not eat anything as no one was ravenous, and they always had to save what little food they had for the rest of the journey.

Day 2

After an insufficient amount of sleep, the team was not ready for another day of continuous running and hiding. They still got up and packed up all their things. While double-checking their bags, Ray found the piece of parasium he had taken from Professor. He picked it up to examine it like anyone would do.

The moment he touched it, he shut down, quite literally, And then got back up. But something was off about him. His eyes had gone black, and two purple lines were on either side of his face. Out of nowhere and without warning, Ray attacked one of the demons viciously. Everyone else was alarmed by what he was doing and started to defend the demon. Ray almost impaled Tara, but Edward caught the staff, and Chris destroyed the piece of parasium.

With a deep inhale, Ray came back to his senses. Turns out, Professor had used a spell to bewitch the piece of palladium before they left him so that whenever someone touched it, it would temporarily force them to attack the demons. The amount of power that the old man held is scary.

After taking a few deep breaths and sips of water, they crushed the piece of parasium, buried it in the soil, hoping it would not be found again, and resumed their journey again. They left the small cave and raced across the plain.

After fifteen minutes, they advanced to a new biome and the plains that were only grass soon started to show small trees. After more running, the trees grew in size and quantity until they reached a new biome. This one was kind enough to give them trees and wild fruit to conceal the demons.

On top of that, there were water streams interchanging between thick and narrow, and they could drink it. The one thing that creeped them out was the sounds of animals they would hear at random intervals.

Anyways they kept dashing through the land with a few water breaks. At one point, they heard a howl; the only problem was that it was gradually becoming louder. It became more concerning when they heard footsteps and the rustling of leaves. The team stopped and drew their weapons, readying themselves for anything and listened closely to the sounds.

They couldn't hear anything for a moment, and suddenly, a pack of around 4 - 5 wolves leaped onto them. They were caught by surprise and didn't have time to react. Logan didn't have a problem, though. He gave a 'small' punch and sent the wolf flying. Quite a sad thing to witness, but the wolf asked for it.

The other members of the pack were furious and pounced on Logan. Tara shot one of her arrows and missed (on purpose). It was enough for a minor distraction and slowed the wolves down. Logan saw the opportunity and moved away. It was hard to believe that a team of trained demon fighters and four demons were struggling against a pack of wolves.

One of the demons slashed two of the wolves, although he intended to hit only one. The wolves decided it was best to retreat, and the fight ended with two wolves with minor wounds. By the time their fight with the wolves ended, it was already getting dark, so they decided to camp in a small clearing for the night. They didn't light a fire to avoid drawing attention toward them.

Day 3

If The team continued at the same pace, they would reach their destination by evening. For hopefully the last time, they packed up all their things and resumed their journey, and of course, they had a slight berry break before leaving the biome.

The team moved forward, left the lush biome, and entered a new one. This time, there wasn't much green. Instead, it was primarily gray and black in a few spots. The team had reached the foot of Mt. Magni. They didn't realize how big of a climb it was until they looked up. They would not enjoy this.

The team didn't really have a choice, so they climbed up. The ancient civilizations were nice enough to make a path around the mountain that led upward, even if it was a little eroded now. They used the path to climb the mountain; needless to say, it was a lot easier than moving at ninety degrees.

While climbing higher, the team was faced with jagged rocks, some of which were sharp and sturdy enough to crack a boulder. They moved with caution. The air was starting to get thinner, and it was getting difficult to breathe. They stopped to catch their breath and eat something. They heard a bleating sound out of nowhere, and they already knew what was coming. Logan got up and locked his feet in such a position that even a boulder could not make him move.

Chris was perplexed but decided to play along. A moment later, they heard another bleat, and then a mountain goat rammed into Logan. Logan caught the goat by the horns and pushed it away. Goats are really stubborn, so it came back for another round.

This time, Edward locked one of his swords in the gap in the goat's horn (the goat was not harmed). Logan gave the goat a hit on the head, just soft enough to call it a warning hit which was enough for the goat because it ran away right after while giving one more bleat, this time sounding a little louder.

They decided it was a good idea to move faster with fewer breaks, even if breathing was laborious. After an hour of walking along the path, they reached the top of the mountain. They could not believe what they were seeing when they moved past the last bit of rocks.

The team was greeted by the sight of a once grand magestic ring which stood as a portal to the demon world. However, this great portal had suffered a fate of fragmentation. It's once seamless circle sat shattered, its pieces strewn across the ground in an intricate puzzle of broken dreams.

Besides this shattered doorway stood two towering pillars, their forms worn and weathered by the cruelty of mother nature and the relentless passage of time. Crackes marred their surface and ruined their seamless and intricate design and embraced them as if in gentle, creeping decay. The ancient stones, once proud and towering, now bore the marks of erosion, as though they had borne the weight of ages.

A tapestry of vines adorned these pillars, their tendrils weaving a web of nature's embrace. These verdant shrouds concealed the very runes that had once adorned the pillars, rendering their ancient script a mystery to the beholder. The words etched in stone were now veiled by the embrace of living greenery, their secrets known only to the past and the silence of time.

Beneath their feet, the platform itself told a tale of age and wear. The once-smooth surface was now a mosaic of cracks, a roadmap of time's relentless march. Each fissure seemed to tell a story of its own, each line and mark a chapter in the platform's journey through the eons.

At each corner of the platform stood small pillars, unassuming yet sturdy, rising to about three feet in height. Beside each stood a pair of rings, like silent sentinels of a forgotten era. These unpretentious structures, guardians of a world now lost, added a touch of quiet dignity to the scene.

And as the group stepped onto the platform, a sense of melancholy settled over them. The scene was one of faded grandeur, a tapestry of decay and the inexorable march of time. Yet, even in its decline, there was an echo of something powerful, something that had once stood as a testament to the heights of creation.

The demons explained to the humans that this was the only connection between the human world and the demon world and that The Leader severed it by casting a spell. The only way to clean up this mess is for "the boy," whoever he may be, to chant the spell that will repair the portal.

Ray realized that the only person who could successfully reopen the portal was Edward, so he handed the book over to him. Edward admitted that he had never chanted a spell before, and because of this, he was unsure of his ability to perform the task. However, this talent was already inherent in his character; he only needed to trust his instincts.

He made an attempt, but he was at a loss for words. The demons gave him a few prompts, but they weren't sure what the spell said. Then Edward went silent for a moment. He then drew in a deep breath before beginning the chanting that was part of the ritual.

As he continued to recite it, a purple color appeared in his eyes.

When he was finished, the pieces of the portal frame picked themselves up and joined together, the moss covering the ground and pillars began to slowly disappear, and the pillars repaired the broken bits in the portal. The smaller pillars located in the four corners of the ground began to glow, and the two rings behind them floated on top of the pillar in an atom-like formation to create a blue orb in the center of the rings. The portal was illuminated, and the runes began to emit a glowing light. In the very center of the portal, there was a whirlpooling mass of a million shades of blue, green and white. It looked like a dream.

The only thing left to do at this point was for the demons to return to their world. After ascending the few steps in front of the portal, the four demons turned their attention to the group of humans who had assisted them on this journey. They had no idea that they would be working alongside human beings, which was the most exciting part of their journey.

Throughout human history, humans and demons collaborated for the second time. After giving them one last thank you, they stepped through the portal and disappeared into it. They did this without knowing what had happened to the demon world. And with that, they had reached the end of their trip.

After enduring another perilous journey, the group eventually returned to their native land. However, this time, they made it there in just two days rather than three because they could better navigate the various landscapes they encountered.

The group traveled to Edward's school, where they engaged in combat with Professor to examine his body. He was miraculously alive, but only by the skin of his teeth.

His heartbeat and breaths slowed down, and he appeared to be losing consciousness as his eyes began to close. Edward intended to bury him in the vicinity of the school at some point.

Edward located a suitable burial spot while Logan transported Professor there. They dug a pit for Professor to spend the rest of eternity in, and before they laid him down in it, Edward cursed Professor for lying to him the entire time and using him to finish what he couldn't. They are getting ready to leave when Edward notices a book near where they discovered Professor. He moves closer to it and then realizes that it is the book he was not permitted to read then. His interest was piqued, and the result was that Edward felt compelled to open the book. So he did.

The document started off with a preface

"Dear son Edward," it read, and Edward was startled to see his name in the book's very first line. "Dear son Edward," it read.

"My friend and I have both passed away by the time you are reading this."

Edward has just realized that his father was the one who wrote this preface, and as a result, he has started shedding tears. According to the preface, the Professor and Hunt were close friends, and both of them were the last of their lineage to be able to capture demons. This information is given to him.

He discovers that Edward and the other team members are obligated to end a conflict and that the first step in this process is to open the portal, which they have already done. The not-so-good news, however, was that a war would eventually break out, and this group would be responsible for ending it.

His father also mentioned that Professor knew something of this nature would occur. Despite this, Hunt continued to hold out hope that the war could be avoided if Edward remained hidden. The Professor proposed an alternative course of action. There will come a time when neither Professor nor Hunt will be available to Edward, and at that point, he will have no one to instruct him.

Both the Professor and Hunt anticipated that this would take place, so they decided to write the book in a language unknown to the inhabitants of this world. It was Irtese all along.

CHAPTER SIX

THE WAR OF THE DAMNED

Edward realized that his father and the Professor were close friends and the last people alive who possessed the power to conjure spells, trap demons, and who knows what else. Edward is both disheartened and conflicted as a result of the fact that he was unaware of any of this. His hostility for Professor had subsided, but it was still present.

He reflected on his father. The reason why his father was usually busy was because he was working at Professor's laboratory alongside him. Now, everything made perfect sense to him. Ray, immersed in his thoughts at the time, saw that Edward was looking dejected and decided to go and chat with him about it. He convinces Edward that he will be the one to bring an end to the conflict, which serves as motivation for Edward to go on. Unexpectedly, this made him feel much better overall.

As Edward reads through the book that his father and the Professor have given him, he unearths tidbits of essential information to know if they will have any chance of defeating the demons. Additionally, he read about the story Ryu had related to him and the rest of the squad.

However, demons sampled human blood at one point because an animal attack caused someone to bleed while the demons were nearby.

The demons eventually concluded that consuming human blood gave them an advantage. In half an hour, the demons who drank blood became more powerful. Demons immediately began their pursuit of human prey after this point. Edward is told of the first human who seized control of the book and closed the portal, preventing the apocalypse from destroying humanity.

The book also said that a demon could only traverse the portal into the demon world. In the severe conditions of the demon world, a human can't stay alive. The problem is that neither the Professor nor Edward's father knew how Edward would transition into the domain of the demons.

During this time, all demons in the demon realm felt the intense energy of Runar's return to power as it powered up its portal ring and emitted its majestic blue rays of light like it once did. They had spent the previous ten thousand years looking forward to this time and preparing themselves for it.

The demons were preparing to wage war on the human population as they prepared. Putting on their armor while simultaneously sharpening their weapons in preparation for battle. They were armed with anything and everything conceivable, including ballistae, catapults, spears, war hammers, and swords, among other things. However, these were not the typical types of weapons that humans employed. Before being put to use, a variety of spells were cast upon these items, which had been crafted by the demons using their expertise and their metal.

Their destruction has never been surpassed in the annals of human history. However, a few demons are over a thousand years old. These demons are known as "Elders," they are considered wise and respected greatly. The Elders offer the leader of the demons some counsel to stop the attack. There have been instances in the past where humans and demons have fought each other, but the outcomes of those battles have always favored humans.

In response to the inquiry made by the Elders, the leader informed them that the humans' most skilled fighters had either passed away or reached old age. No one is present to aid the humans in this battle, and the leader assured the Elders victory. The argument that the leader of the demons presented was very compelling, and it was sufficient to win over the support of the Elders.

The team is brainstorming ways by which Edward could enter the demon world. Everyone knew that the sort of difficulties the demon world presents is too harsh for a human to survive there. Since no one could devise a plan, Ray pitched his idea. He said he had no idea why he was cursed with his half-demon abilities by an encounter long ago. He suggests that it was preparing him for this moment. It will be Ray who will go into the demon world to bring back the book. The team was initially reluctant but realized it was their only option, so they eventually agreed.

They knew that Edward would eventually stop the demons, but they needed that book to guide them. When everyone was on board with the idea of Ray retrieving the book, each member was assigned a role. Since Edward and Logan had the largest skillset and strength, they would take the demons head-on.

They would try to hold them off for as long as possible while Ray enters the portal. Tara, one of the smart ones, was assigned as the trap master. She has to make traps and enclosures to contain the demons, even for a little while. Chris will support humans, defend their homes and families, and assist in necessary evacuations. Now, of course, many do not know that demons exist or that a war will occur in a matter of hours. They will find out soon enough, but right now, they're going in blind. Ray left for Runar immediately to make it in time for the ambush.

Ray makes the trip to Runar for the third time, leaving a little earlier to ensure he arrives on time. The sky became a scarlet color that was almost black, and a thick layer of clouds began to cover the entire sky. It was getting close to the hour when the battle would begin. His trip was going very well, and he was making excellent progress at a higher rate than ever.

By this point, he had the route to Runar almost wholly committed to memory. He was moving at a constant and rapid pace, which was sufficient to allow him to get to the portal on time; nevertheless, he was suddenly sidetracked by something he was unprepared to witness. Ray navigated around a massive boulder that was in his path.

He was taken aback when he spotted two demons approaching the city. This indicated that the demons had already started their invasion, which posed a significant risk to everyone because no one had anticipated that a demon would launch an attack so quickly. There was still work on the defenses, and nobody was entirely ready. This would create a significant obstacle. Despite this, Ray used his staff to kill both demons and continued on his journey with a worried mindset.

Ray had traveled almost eight more hours before arriving at the gateway. It was just a matter of time before he could read the book. Ray climbed up the imposing staircase to the platform of the luminous blue door. A buzzing began just as he was about to enter the portal, and it immediately turned green. A human being emerged from the opening one second later.

Ray was surprised, and as a result, he retreated. The human's clothing was torn to shreds, his face was red with blood, and his limbs were covered in scars. Ashes were caught in his hair, and he was wheezing as he tried to get some air into his lungs. He barely clung to life by a thread. Ray attempted to get his response, but all the human could do was struggle to breathe.

He successfully gathered every last bit of energy he had left in him and then informed Ray about the book's location, with the expectation that Ray would read, comprehend, and make use of the book. After relaying this knowledge to Ray, the man closed his eyes and breathed his last breath before passing away. There was nothing that Ray could have done to prevent the death of the other man.

Ray stepped through the portal with wet eyes and immediately found himself in the demonic domain. It was precisely how he had imagined it would be. The sky was crimson and fully shrouded over with storm clouds.

The ground was covered with slimy vines, the trees had so few leaves that Ray could count them, and ash was flying everywhere. His sight was tinged with a crimson color. There were no indications of life everywhere, but he saw a bunker colored purple and black not too far away from where he was standing.

Ray hurried in its direction, but he quickly saw that it wasn't just a bunker; instead, it was an entire complex of shacks with blacksmith bellows, armament, armor, and various other types of war weapons. Ray was taken aback by the appearance of the firearms and ammunition. When he turned his head to the right, he noticed a hole at least 5 meters in diameter and contained a hammer inside it.

He deduced that the crater had been caused by the hammer, and as a result, he realized that the humans were in a significantly more perilous situation than they had believed. Who knows what other devices and gizmos the demons had concocted, but if they had a whole weapon house full of these hammers, they could create mass havoc with just a few strokes and do it with just a few blows.

This incentivized him to finish the assignment as quickly as possible. Ray saw a horde of demons charging straight toward him as they approached. He hid himself behind a shack in the hopes of avoiding detection. He noticed they were heading toward the gateway, which could only indicate one thing: the demons had started their assault.

The news was highly upsetting, but Ray had no choice but to continue. He saw a peculiar building made of Blackstone with purple ores lining it. Filled with curiosity, Ray entered the building. He didn't see anyone. Only a pedestal on which a black and purple box was kept. He advanced toward the box and lifted the lid. He was looking at the book Edward was supposed to use to end the war.

His heart beating faster than it ever had, he picked up the book and immediately dropped it excitedly. He collected his overflowing emotions and dashed out the door when he was stopped in his tracks by a demon which wasn't much of a surprise.

This time, the demon he had to fight was much more brutal than the two he met on the way to the portal. This one could swap places with any living being close to it, which made it frustrating to wound it. Any attack Ray would throw at it, the demon would swap places, and he would just end up attacking nothing.

He ended up getting hit by the demon's club on his arm. He felt something dislocate; however, he had to continue fighting. Ray barely dodged the attacks by a hair and forced his dislocated elbow back into place. He let out a shriek and fell down. He was now in a vulnerable position, open to any attacks. The demon didn't waste his golden opportunity and swung his club and Ray.

By some miracle, Ray's left arm charged up with some sort of energy, swung itself at the club, and broke it with splinters flying past Ray. He looked at his arm. It was green and black. He realized it was a demonic ability. He could use it since he was half demon. It's hard to believe how one limb can cause such a massive difference in a fight. Ray now had a considerable advantage.

He decided to use the demon as a testing device for his newly acquired power which is probably what anyone would have done. He charged up his arm once more and aimed for the demon's chest to hit its heart and end the battle. And it is no surprise that he succeeded.

Ray pulled his arm out of the demon, covered in purple blood. The demon fell down and turned into purple dust. Ray grabbed the book and dashed toward the portal. That fight was a considerable delay in his journey back to aid the others.

The scene was chaotic and grim as the demons ravaged the human world. Despite their efforts, Edward and Logan were only managing to hold their own against the onslaught. Meanwhile, Tara had cleverly trapped a group of demons while Chris led the disoriented humans to safety. However, the situation became dire when the primary defenses were breached due to Ray's theft of the book and escape through the portal. The demons detected a disturbance and immediately rushed toward the portal, leaving the team with no time to spare.

With the demons closing in, Ray decided to hide among the nearby structures and devise a plan. He waited for hours until the demons finally arrived, then quickly retreated back into the portal undetected. The team reunited with Ray, and he handed over the book, informing Edward that a specific spell needed to be read aloud.

The spell was written in an unfamiliar language, causing Edward to panic as he had no prior experience or training in casting such spells. Nevertheless, he chanted the spell with a heavy heart, fearing the consequences of his actions.

At first, nothing appeared to happen, but gradually, the portal lost its luster, and the runes and gems began to fade away. The team erupted in ecstatic jubilation and celebrated their success with a group hug centered around Edward. Afterward, they pondered what to do with the book, knowing the catastrophic consequences it could cause if it fell into the wrong hands. They ultimately decided to burn the book, but to their surprise, it was protected by a spell that prevented it from catching fire.

Determined to destroy the book, Edward remembered a de-enchanting spell taught to him by a professor. He recited the spell, focusing his energy on the book, and successfully removed all its curses and enchantments. As a result, the book caught fire and was reduced to ashes, which the team collected in a box made of iron and discarded into the ocean, ensuring that it would never be found by man or demon again.

Now that they had completed their mission, the team returned home to celebrate. Edward could not stop thinking about his father and Professor. He realized the Professor only wanted to keep the world safe by killing the last demons on Earth.

CHAPTER SEVEN

Sir Edward Hunt

8 years later

It's been eight years since the war was resolved, and Edward decided to visit his childhood home where his parents died. He drove across urban and downtown areas and entered the suburbs on the outskirts of the country with his wife and daughter. After spotting his childhood home, Edward hesitated before leaving the car.

Memories of his parents flooded back to him. Tears roll down his eyes, but he is comforted by his family. He didn't want to go inside the house, so they all left. They have a nice meatloaf dinner at his new home, where he and his family live. Later in the night, he finds his wife cleaning the kitchen. He took his daughter to her bed and told her stories about his adventures with his team and how he fought the demons and closed the portal. But she doesn't know it was he who accomplished the feats.

In Edward's stories, a team of brave warriors ended the war. When he is done narrating his epic to his daughter, he leaves the room. As Edward tucked his daughter into bed, she looked up at him with big, fearful eyes. "Daddy, can I ask you something?" she whispered.

"Of course, sweetie," he said, settling down beside her.

"I'm scared of the dark," she said. "What if there are monsters like in your stories?"

Edward paused for a moment, considering how to respond.

"Well, sweetie, those stories aren't real," he said at last. "They're just made up. But if it makes you feel better, I can leave the night light on for you."

The following day, the family gathers at the breakfast table, the scent of bacon and eggs filling the air. Edward stares blankly at his plate, lost in thought. His wife and daughter exchange concerned glances but say nothing. After breakfast, they pile into the car and go to the cemetery. The sky is a deep shade of blue, with wispy clouds floating lazily by. As they approach the gravesite, Edward's heart feels heavy. He hasn't been here in years, and the memories come flooding back.

The grass is soft beneath their feet as they reach the gravestone. It's simple, with just the names and dates of birth and death. Edward feels a lump in his throat as he looks at the dates - it's been so long since his parents passed away.

He kneels down and places the flowers on the ground before the gravestone. His wife and daughter stand behind him, hands on his shoulders. Edward looks up at the sky, tears streaming down his face. He feels a deep sense of loss and longing, wishing he could return time and be with his parents again.

His wife and daughter wrap their arms around him, providing comfort and support. It's a bittersweet moment - a chance to honor the memory of his parents but also a painful reminder of what he's lost.

As they return to the car, Edward feels a sense of closure and a lingering ache. In the mix of these mildly negative emotions, he feels an odd peace of mind, knowing that demons or other fantastical creatures will never be seen roaming our little world's various terrains and biomes again.